For Éléonore

I'M Not SydNEy!

MaRie-LouisE Gay

GROUNDWOOD BOOKS
HOUSE OF ANANSI PRESS
TORONTO / BERKELEY

Sydney inched his way along the branch.
The air was warm.
The leaves were rustling.
"Sydney!" called Sami. "Where are you?"

"Here," he answered, in a soft, slow voice. "But I'm not
Sydney. I am a sloth."

"Oh?" Sami looked up.

The leaves and flowers unfurled.

Birds of every color flew through the tropical forest.

The sloth's fur glistened in the sun.

"I think I might chew on a nice juicy leaf," he said.

Sami laughed.

"A sloth is so lazy. It does nothing all day," she said.

"Not true," drawled the sloth. "I smile. I sleep. I daydream. My days are full."

"A sloth is way too slow," said Sami. "I would rather be a spider monkey."

Before the sloth could blink an eye, Sami scampered up the tree.

The spider monkey leaped from branch to branch,
curling and uncurling her long, skinny tail.
Her round eyes darted here and there looking for fresh fruit.
Leaves scattered in the air.
Startled hummingbirds flew every which way.
"You are making me dizzy," the sloth grumbled softly. "You
are going too fast."
"Fast is fun!" chattered the spider monkey. "Fast is best!"

"Hey!" Edward called from below. "What are you two doing?"
"Can't you see?" squealed the spider monkey. "I am a spider monkey, and he is a sloth."
"Well, well," said Edward. "How about that?"

Then Edward smiled. A wide elephantine smile.
He got down on all fours and almost disappeared
into the tall, waving grass.
The sun shone warmly on his back. Grasshoppers
chirped in his ears.

The elephant's trunk swayed back and forth
as he lumbered slowly across the savanna.
The earth shook.
His huge ears flapped like giant flags in the
wind.
The yellow grass smelled of burnt toast and
red earth.

"I'M THE KING OF THE SAVANNA!" trumpeted
the elephant.
The sloth and the spider monkey almost fell out of the tree.
"Whoooooah!" said the sloth. "Calm down! Life is too short
to make such a fuss."
The sloth yawned hugely.
The king of the savanna roared with laughter.

Anamaria was walking along when she heard strange noises.
She looked up.
"What are you doing?" Anamaria asked.
"Oh, we're just hanging around …" answered the sloth,
smiling sweetly.
"… and monkeying about," giggled the spider monkey.
"I'm eating some nice fresh tree bark," said the elephant.

"Well, well," said Anamaria. "I'm sort of hungry, too."
She crouched down and shuffled along in the sand,
raising little puffs of golden dust.
Her nose twitched as she sniffed this way and that.
"Something smells awfully delicious," she said and
stuck out her tongue.

Yuck!

Slurrp! The anteater scooped up a huge bunch of ants.

"What are you doing?" cried the spider monkey.

"I'm eating lunch," answered the anteater.

"You eat *ants*?" she squealed. "Yuck!"

"I am an *ant*-eater!"

"I don't eat spiders!" said the spider monkey.

"How about termites?" asked the anteater. "Have you tried termite teriyaki?"

"Double-yuck!" shrieked the monkey. "Yuckity-yuck!"

Slurrp!

"Be quiet!" squeaked Brigitte.
Everybody looked up. No one had heard or seen Brigitte arrive.
But there she was, hanging upside down,
her velvety, dusty wings wrapped around her tiny furry body.
Her large ears quivered.
"I hunted mosquitoes all night," said the bat.
"I must have eaten at least six thousand.
I'm full and I'm tired. I want to sleep."
She closed her eyes.

"That's impossible!" cried the anteater.

"I can eat three hundred thousand ants a day. But you're so tiny.
How could you possibly eat so many mosquitoes in one night?"

"I do!" squeaked the bat. "I just do!"

She was upset. Nobody ever believed her.

The little bat dove and swooped around everybody's heads.
"Stop tickling me," said the sloth, trying to bat the bat away.
The anteater shook her long snout and sneezed.
The spider monkey bounced around like a ping-pong ball.
The elephant got very annoyed. He filled his trunk with water,
took aim at the tiny bat and …

I do!

... WHOOOOOSH!
Edward roared with laughter.
So did Brigitte, Sydney, Sami
and Anamaria!

Just then, they heard their mothers and fathers calling out,
"Time for supper!"
The children galloped home like a herd of small wet animals ...

That evening, Sydney fell asleep on a pile of fresh juicy leaves while his sister Anamaria licked her plate clean.

That evening, Sami scampered up the stairs and took a
flying leap into her bed.
And Edward splished and splashed around in the bath ...

But Brigitte couldn't sleep.
It was time to fly out into the night.

Published in 2022 by Groundwood Books / House of Anansi Press
groundwoodbooks.com

Groundwood Books respectfully acknowledges that the land on which we operate is the Traditional Territory of many Nations, including the Anishinabeg, the Wendat and the Haudenosaunee. It is also the Treaty Lands of the Mississaugas of the Credit.

We gratefully acknowledge for their financial support of our publishing program the Canada Council for the Arts, the Ontario Arts Council and the Government of Canada.

Library and Archives Canada Cataloguing in Publication
Title: I'm not Sydney! / Marie-Louise Gay.
Other titles: I am not Sydney!
Names: Gay, Marie-Louise, author, illustrator.
Identifiers: Canadiana (print) 20210231572 | Canadiana (ebook) 20210231580 | ISBN 9781773065977 (hardcover) | ISBN 9781773065984 (EPUB) | ISBN 9781773065991 (Kindle)
Classification: LCC PS8563.A868 I42 2022 | DDC jC813/.54—dc23

The illustrations were done in watercolor, 6B pencil and opaque white ink.
Design by Michael Solomon
Printed and bound in South Korea